My Dad's the Queen of All VTubers?!

1

Presented by
Wataru Akashingo

Contents

My Dad's the Queen of All VTubers?!
Presented by Akashingo Wataru

VTuber

An online entertainer, typically represented by a 2D or 3D digital avatar.

BROAD
1
CAST

HEH... KIZUKE YAI'S SO GODDAMN CUTE...
HIHIII AND HEWWO EVERY-ONE! IT'S YAI TIME, KYUN! ☆
I KNOW A LOT OF VTUBERS ARE DUDES, BUT THE RUMORS SAY YAI-CHAN'S THE REAL DEAL. AN ACTUAL CUTE GIRL BEHIND THE SCREEN...
TAKASHI, DINNER'S READY. COULD YOU GET YOUR FATHER?
FIIINE.
TSK... THE VIDEO WAS JUST GETTING GOOD, TOO.
CLICK
HEY DAD, DINNER'S-
WE DID LOTS AND LOTS TODAY! THAT'S ALL FROM YOUR SWEETIE FOR NOW~ ☆
8888888
I love you!!
Kyunkyuun!!
Yai-chaaa
THANKIES FOR TUNING IN, EVERY-KYUN~!☆ SEE YOU NEXT-
OH.

What happened, Yai-kyun?!
Is somebody there?
AUUUUGH!!
AUU......
EEEEEEK!!
FWAP
WH-WHAT THE HELL IS THIS, DA—
PING!
Was that a guy's voice just now?
PING!
N-No way!
PING!
Yai-kyun's boyfriend, maybe?!

N-NO WAAAY! YOU KNOW YAI'S EVERYONE'S SWEETHEART, REMEMBER?
I DON'T HAVE A BOYFRIEND, SILLIES! ☆
WHAT THE HELL IS THIS?
MY DAD'S A REGULAR GUY WITH AN OFFICE JOB...
HE'S AN EARNEST FAMILY MAN, A HARD WORKER...
THAT'S HOW I'VE ALWAYS KNOWN HIM, BUT...
Just roll with me here! Play the part of my big brother. I'll explain later!
Just roll with me here! Play the part of my big brother. I'll explain later!
DAD?!
HEY BIG BWO!
CAN YOU TELL ALL MY VIEWERS THAT YOU'RE SO HAPPY THEY'VE BEEN FOLLOWING YOUR PRECIOUS WIDDLE SISTER? ☆
DAD?!

...I'M, UH... I'M REALLY HAPPY YOU'VE BEEN FOLLOWING MY PRECIOUS WIDDLE SISTER YAI-KYUN... PLEASE... PLEASE KEEP WATCHING HER VIDEOS...
DAD...
SEE? YAI-KYUN'S SO HAPPY FOR ALL YOUR SUPPORT, BOYS! THANKIES! SEE YOU SOON, KYUN! ☆
DAAAAAD!!
AAAAAAAGH!!
GLOOM
GLOOM
YOU TWO OKAY? YOU'VE BARELY SAID A WORD.
?
...
JUST FINE, KYUN ...
TWITCH
KYUN?

THE CUTE VIRTUAL GIRL I'VE HAD A CRUSH ON ALL THIS TIME...
IS MY DAD.
S-SO UH... VTUBING, HUH? THAT'S... GREAT...
I, UH... HM... WELL... HM...
J-JUST STOP, SON... DON'T HUMOR ME...
HOW DID YOU EVEN KEEP THIS A SECRET?
I'VE BEEN DOING IT WHILE YOU AND YOUR MOM WERE OTHERWISE OCCUPIED...
I QUIT MY OFFICE JOB. THIS HAS BEEN MY SOLE SOURCE OF INCOME FOR A WHILE NOW.
KYUN!
WH-WHAAAAAT?!

SON... MY PANTY SHOTS HAVE BEEN PUTTING FOOD ON OUR TABLE FOR MONTHS.
KYUN☆
PLEASE STOP, I BEG OF YOU!
THIS IS WRONG, DAD! IT'S NOT RIGHT! YOU CAN'T DO THIS!
IT'S FINE, SON. YOUR DAD'S QUITE THE POPULAR FIGURE AT THIS POINT.
I'M WELL AWARE OF THAT. THAT'S NOT WHAT I MEANT!
TO BE HONEST, I'VE BEEN LOVING EVERY MINUTE OF IT.
SOME PEOPLE EVEN SEND IN THEIR OWN FANMADE SONGS AND CREATIONS!
ONE GUY EVEN TOLD ME "YOU'RE MY FIRST CRUSH! BUT I'LL LOVE YOU FOREVER!"
WAIT. THAT WAS ME. NOOOOO! NOT LIKE THIS!

THAT'S WHY I SAY "KYUN," YOU KNOW...
IT'S THE ONLY WAY I CAN VERBALIZE THAT FUZZY FEELING I GET WHEN I STREAM...THE KIND OF FEELING I HAVEN'T HAD SINCE I FIRST LAID EYES ON YOUR MOTHER.
I DON'T WANNA HEAR IT!
I'VE HEARD ENOUGH! I'M NEVER GONNA UNDER-STAND, AND I'M NOT SURE I WANT TO!
I'M TELLING MOM WE'VE GOT AN UNEMPLOYED 40-YEAR-OLD KYUN-KYUN WEIRDO LIVING IN THE HOUSE!!
W-WAIT! I'M ONLY 39!
I DON'T CARE!!
STOMP
MOM! DAD'S-
WHAM

CUT THE SHIT! I ALREADY SAID I'M NOT A GUY!
"KIZUKE YAI IS TOTALLY WIFE MATERIAL, YOU COULD LEARN A THING OR TWO FROM HER"?! UP YOURS, PAL!
I'M AN ETER-NALLY 17-YEAR-OLD IDOL AND I'M NOT-HUH?!
MY VIEWER-SHIP DROPPED TO ZERO?! WHAT THE HELL?!
THIS IS BULL! HOW AM I MEANT TO COM-PETE?
KIZUKE YAI FANS ARE TRASH! TOTAL TRASH!

SORRY YOU HAD TO SEE THAT ...
GROAN...
THAT WAS QUITE THE SURPRISE, TAKASHI.
PLONK
UHH... HUH...
IN MY YOUNGER DAYS, I WAS ACTUALLY AN ASPIRING IDOL...BUT I GAVE UP ON THAT DREAM AFTER GETTING MARRIED.
ONE DAY I HAPPENED TO CATCH A KIZUKE YAI STREAM, AND SEEING HER REKINDLED MY OLD PASSION.
DAD ...!
BUT HONESTLY, SCREW THAT SO-CALLED "VTUBER QUEEN"... YOU JUST KNOW SHE'S SOME SEEDY OLD MAN GAMING THE SYSTEM!
KYUN!☆
I DON'T WANT TO FALL BEHIND SOME WEIRDO SELLING PANTY SHOTS TO PERVERTS, YOU KNOW?!

IT'S NOT LIKE I WANT THAT MANY FANS OR ANYTHING... JUST A TENTH OF YAI'S WOULD BE FINE.
SIGH...
YEAH. I'D BE HAPPY JUST HAVING AROUND 100,000 SUB-SCRIBERS. I THINK I'D BE ABLE TO QUIT AND SAY I DID A GOOD JOB IF THAT HAPPENED.
"JUST" 100,000 ?!
DAD'S A NATIONALLY RENOWNED IDOL SEN-SATION!
THIS IS BAD! ONCE MOM SETS HER MIND ON SOME-THING SHE DOESN'T STOP...
THAT SEEDY OLD MAN IS YOUR HUSBAND, MOM! HOW AM I SUP-POSED TO TELL YOU THAT?!
DAMN IT! I DON'T HAVE A CHOICE ...
I DON'T HAVE A GODDAMN CHOICE!
DASH

DAD!
WHAM
TWITCH
WH-WHAT? DID YOU FINISH TELLING YOUR MOTHER?
U-UHM... ACTUALLY, NEVERMIND ABOUT THAT... I, UH...
HAHA... I'M A LITTLE INTERESTED IN STREAM-ING, MYSELF...
SHUDDER
SHUDDER
S-SAY, UH... WHAT'S THE BEST WAY TO EARN SUB-SCRIBERS, ANYWAY? HAHA...
THINK YOU'VE GOT WHAT IT TAKES TO TOP YOUR OLD MAN, EH?
I CAN'T SAY IT WON'T BE ROUGH, KYUN!
GLARE
I HATE EVERY BIT OF THIS.

WELL. I GUESS I'M MY DAD'S APPREN-TICE(?) NOW.
OBVIOUSLY I DON'T CARE ABOUT GAINING SUBSCRIBERS. I DON'T CARE ABOUT STREAMING, EITHER.
STAGE 1: LEARN DAD'S VTUBING TRICKS SO I CAN HELP MOM RAISE HER SUB COUNT.
STAGE 2: FIGURE OUT A WAY TO MAKE DAD RETIRE BEFORE I START BLEEDING FROM MY EYES.
FOR THE SAKE OF MY PLAN, I'LL GRIN AND BEAR IT FOR NOW...
WIGGLE
IT'LL BE OKAY! I'LL WALK THROUGH THE FIRES OF THIS HELL. I'LL COME OUT THE OTHER SIDE AS A STRONGER MAN!
I'LL STEEL MY HEART AND—
THANKIES, EVERYONE! NOW IT'S TIME FOR MY BIG PERFOR-MANCE, KYUN~! ☆

KYUN-KYUUUN! LOOK, LOOK! ONE OF MY FANS WROTE A SONG FOR ME! WOWIE! ☆
I THOUGHT IT'D BE FUN IF I DID A SPECIAL YAI-KYUN DANCE, WHAT DO YOU THINK~? ☆
WAIT ...
SOME PEOPLE EVEN SEND IN THEIR OWN FAN-MADE SONGS ...
NO... PLEASE DON'T TELL ME IT'S MY SONG ...
W-WAIT-!!
NOOOOOOOOOOOOOOOOOOO!!
SWISH
WELL, LET'S START THE SONG! ☆
BEEP!

"YOU'RE JUST SO KYUN-KYUN"
VOCALS, DANCE: KIZUKE YAI
LYRICS: TKS
KYUN-KYUN, KYUN-KYUN
L-O-V-E KYUN-KYUN!
WHAT SECRETS HIDE BEHIND THAT EXPRESSION? ♫
I'VE BEEN THINKING OF YOU, YOU'VE MADE QUITE THE IMPRESSION... ♪
MY HEART GOES KYUN-KYUN, BEATING OUT OF MY CHEST. ♫

BEFORE I EVEN KNEW IT, I'D BEEN PUT TO THE TEST.
THERE'S SOME-THING ABOUT YOU, SOME-THING I CAN'T SHAKE...
YOUR FAMILIAR FACE, IT KEEPS ME AWAKE!
IF I CAN'T SEE YOU SMILING, MY HEART'LL JUST BREAK!
THOSE CHER-ISHED OLD MEM-ORIES, DEEP IN MY SOUL!
SOME-TIMES IT FEELS LIKE THEY'RE NO LONGER WHOLE...
BUT. EVEN. SOOOOO...

I'LL WIPE MY EYES! DRY MY TEARS! ♪ KIZUKE'S HERE, NO TIME FOR FEARS! ♪ (KYUN-KYUN KYUN-KYUN PARADISE!)
LIKE A SHIP LOST AT SEA, I'VE FOUND PEACE ON YOUR SHORES! KIZUKE YAI, MY HEART IS YOUUUUUURS! (L-O-V-E SHE'S SO NICE! ☆)
AFTER THAT... INCI-DENT... I TRIED TEACHING MOM TO DANCE LIKE DAD.
HUH?
UHH...
LIKE THIS?
OH CRAP...
MOM NEVER SHUT UP ABOUT HOW HER EQUIPMENT COULDN'T KEEP UP WITH HER MOVEMENT, AND AS A RESULT HER SUB COUNT STAYED AT A BIG FAT ZERO.
THUS, WE STILL HAD 100,000 MORE TO GO.
TRAGI-CALLY, TAKASHI'S PATH OF SUFFERING HAD ONLY JUST BEGUN.
BROADCAST #1:END

GOOD WORK (AT THE OFFICE) TODAY, HONEY.
I CAN ONLY WORK SO HARD (AS A VTUBER) THANKS TO YOU, SWEETHEART ...
"OH LOOK AT ME. KYUN-KYUN UWU." WHO'S THIS HUSSY TRYING TO FOOL, HUH?!
SHE MIGHT HAVE EVERYONE FOOLED WITH THAT SHITTY "I'M A SMOL BEAN TEE-HEE, OOPSIES YOU SAW MY PANTIES!" ROUTINE, BUT I JUST KNOW SHE'S SOME SHITTY OLD UNEMPLOYED DUDE WITH NO LIFE!!
You're so cuuute!
Yai time!
Yai-kyuuuun!
888888
You're so girly!

My Dad's the Queen of All VTubers?!

SO...MY PARENTS ARE VTUBERS. DAD'S A NATIONALLY BELOVED VIRTUAL GIRL, AND MOM'S A TRASH-TIER WANNABE IDOL.
THIS COULD'VE ONLY HAPPENED IN THE INFORMATION ERA! IT'S NOT FAIR! NO MODERN CHILD IS SAFE FROM THE THREAT OF TERMINALLY ONLINE PARENTS!
EAT UP, YOU TWO!
Sizzle
YOU SEEM HAPPY. SOMETHING GOOD HAPPEN AT WORK?
Sizzle
YEP, I'VE GOT A NEW INTERN. HE HAS POTEN-TIAL.
DAD'S PANTY SHOTS PAID FOR THIS...
*(THE INTERN)
BROAD 2 CAST
BRO, YOU CATCH KIZUKE YAI'S LATEST BROAD-CAST?
HELL YEAH.
MESU BUTA
PRFBFRHBHHT

MAN, SHE'S SO GIRLY. YOU CAN TELL SHE'S THE REAL DEAL FROM THE WAY SHE MOVES.
HELL YEAH.
HE'S SO SMUG!
KYUN☆
SOME-THING ON YOUR MIND, HUN?
WELL, HAVE YOU EVER HEARD OF KIZUK-
AUGH
HEY, DAD. I DON'T THINK YOU'VE HAD ENOUGH MEAT.
HERE. HAVE SOME MORE. STUFF YOUR MOUTH WITH IT!!
ISN'T YOUR IDENTITY MEANT TO BE SECRET?!
S-SORRY, I WAS JUST SO HAPPY! ☆
EHEHE. NICE TO SEE YOU BOYS GETTING ALONG!

OH DUDE, YOU SEEN THIS?
IT'S SOME VTUBER NAMED "CRY TEKARI."
MESU BUTA
?!
OOF.
SOME BIG 'OLD DUDE' ENERGY HERE.
YEAH, LOOK AT HIS JANKY-ASS DANCING! AND THE WAY HE ACTS! YOU CAN SMELL HIS GROSS BURP BREATH THROUGH THE SCREEN!
LUL.
Trying to Dance
SIZZLE...
RAGE...
BRAAAP
SHE'S GONNA LOSE IT!!
O-OLD DUDE... ENERGY...?
JANK... JANKY-ASS... DANCING...?
M-MOM! CALM DOWN!
?

I'M A 34-YEAR-OLD WOMAN! I'M STRONG, INDEPENDENT, AND PLENTY FEMININE! WHAT'S THE BIG DEA-
AUGH?!
BASH
MOM?!
AW CRAP!
MOM!!
CLATTER!
OH NO, THE MEAT! I'M SORRY!
DON'T WORRY ABOUT THAT, HUN!
LET ME SEE YOUR HAND... ARE YOU HURT?
YOUR WELL-BEING'S MORE IMPORTANT THAN SOME MEAT, SWEETHEART. HERE, I BROUGHT A BAND-AID.
KYUN
HOLY SHIT... DAD'S TOTALLY WIFE MATERIAL!

HEHEH! FOOD'S MUCH NICER WHEN EATEN WITH FAMILY, AIN'T IT?
SOME-THING LIKE THAT ...
TO BE FAIR, OTHER THAN THE VTUBER STUFF, IT WASN'T ALL THAT BAD...
SO, WHERE TO NEXT? DO YOU WANT TO HIT SOME STORES, MOM-
OH ...
You can be a VTuber!
V
WOW... CAN I BE LIKE HER?
WHAT'S THAT?

"Full Motion Capture"
A smooth, full-body system that captures all of your motions to an accurate degree.
Full MOTION CAPTURE
IF I WANT TO CLOSE THE GAP BETWEEN KIZUKE YAI AND ME...
THEN I JUST NEED THE RIGHT HARDWARE!
NOPE. THAT'S DEFI-NITELY A SOFT-WARE ISSUE!
You can be a VTuber!
WH– MOM! YOU'RE BETTER THAN THIS! DON'T FALL FOR THE SIREN SONG!
I WAS THINK-ING OF BUYING ONE ANYWAY ...
I'M JUST GOING TO TAKE A LOOK! JUST A PEEK! ♪
W-WAIIIT!!
WAIT, CRAP! IF DAD SEES HER, THEN—
Swish
THAT'S THE WAY, GIRLS!
DON'T FORGET TO SMILE! ☆

DAD, YOU'RE NOT A STAR ATHLETE COACHING A JUNIOR SOCCER TEAM, STOP!
THEY'LL BE THE NEXT GENERATION OF TALENT ...
DUDE, IT'S WEIRD!
MUTTER
MUTTER
THINK ABOUT YOUR SUR-ROUNDINGS! PEOPLE ARE LOOKING!
YEOWCH! THAT'S NO FAIR, TAKASHI!
YOU'RE SUPPOSED TO BE THE PARENT HERE, NOT ME!
DAMN IT! NOW I HAVE TO GO AFTER MOM...
DING
KIZUKE YAI SPECIAL PROMO!

WHAT TAKA-SHI SEES
AUUUUUUGH!!
NOOOO! I DON'T WANT TO SEE IT!
EEEEEEK!!
WHAT'S WRONG, SON? DID YOU SEE SOMETHING TRAU-MATIC?
DO I NEED TO CALL AN EXORCIST?
YEAH. TO BANISH YOU!

SHE'S A GROWN WOMAN... SURELY SHE CAN KEEP HERSELF UNDER CONTROL. RIGHT? RIGHT?!
NOW I JUST GOTTA DEAL WITH MOM ...
AAAHHH...
MASSAGE CHAIRS
I DROPPED OFF DAD AT THE WAITING AREA AND HEADED INTO THE STORE.
I CAN SEE YOU'RE VERY BEAUTIFUL, MA'AM. I'D SUGGEST THESE ACCESSORIES AND HARDWARE TO HELP BRING OUT YOUR NATURAL RADIANCE IN THE VIRTUAL WORLD.
THE FULL PACKAGE DEAL COMES OUT TO 450,000 YEN!
YEAH!
I'LL TAKE IT!

NOOOO! MOM! I TOLD YOU TO IGNORE THE SIREN SONG! DON'T BELIEVE HIS LIES!
HUH? LIES...? BUT I THOUGHT YOU BE-LIEVED IN ME...
GHH... WAIT, NO! I JUST DON'T THINK IT'S A GOOD INVEST-MENT ...
NONSENSE, FRIEND! WHY, YOUR BEAUTIFUL MOTHER'S VTUBING WILL PAY FOR ITSELF!
BEHOLD... FULL MOTION CAPTURE! A MIRACLE INVESTMENT!
Full MOTION CAPTURE
YOU KNOW AS WELL AS I DO THAT CASUAL KARAOKE DOESN'T MAKE YOU THE KING OF POP!
I'M NOT LETTING YOU DO THIS TO YOURSELF, MOM!
IT'S NOT HAPPEN-ING! YOU CAN'T KEEP GETTING AWAY WITH IT!
I'M SAYING NO! SOMEONE HAS TO PROTECT THIS FAMILY!
UN KO

THANK YOU MA'AM, HAVE A LOVELY DAY.
AH, COULD I ARRANGE DELIVERY?
Here's my card.
I'M POWERLESS... THERE'S NOTHING I CAN DO...
HOPE IT WAS WORTH IT, YOU HAG ...
HOPE YOU GET YOUR DAMN SUBSCRIBERS, CUT THIS OUT, AND THEN WE CAN FORGET THIS EVER HAPPENED ...
SOMETHING UP, SON?
FLINCH
N-NOTHING AT ALL, DAD! WHAT'S UP?
ACTUALLY, I HAVE A PRESENT FOR YOU.

YOU SAID YOU WERE INTERESTED IN STREAMING, SO...
I GOT YOU SOME MOTION CAPTURE EQUIPMENT!
MOTIO CAPTURE
MY DREAM OF A FATHER-SON COLLAB ...
TAKASHI'S LONG TORTURE HAD BARELY EVEN STARTED.
ON THE BRIGHT SIDE, HIS MOM GAINED 50 SUBSCRIBERS.
Not bad, gramps.
JUST 99,950 TO GO!
It's fun to watch old people do this kinda thing.
I love this guy!
Dude your video stinks as bad as your breath.
LMAO. Funny moves, gramps. Very epic. Subscribed.
Clickety-clack
BROADCAST #2: END

DAD'S WORLD
(Special Broadcast: Their Worlds)
MY DAILY LIFE WAS THE SAME, NOTHING CHANGED.
BUT THAT PREDICT-ABILITY DIDN'T LAST.
VTUBERS STARTED TAKING THE WORLD BY STORM, AND NATURALLY I LEARNED ABOUT THEM TOO.
motion capture
BEGIN LIFE ANEW!
YOUR BEAUTIFUL DREAMS CAN COME TRUE!
MY WORLD WAS ROCKED TO ITS CORE.

EVERYTHING UNFURLED, SHOWING ME A REALITY I'D BEEN BLIND TO.
You're so cute!
Kyun Kyun Fall In Love!
You're mega adorable lolololol
I'm here for you!
8888888888
You're my first crush! But
Yai-kyuuuu
Yai-kyun, you're the cutest!
We're rootin
I'm always thinking of you, Yai-kyun!!
VTuber
KIZUKE YAI FAIR!
Every
Kizu
NOW THE WORLD OUTSIDE IS A WHOLE NEW WORLD, ONE I CAN'T UNSEE.
Kizuke Yai Sensatio
KiZUKE YAi
Kizuke Yai fa
THIS IS MY LIFE NOW.

TAKASHI'S REALITY
MY DAILY LIFE WAS THE SAME, NOTHING CHANGED.
BUT THAT PREDICT-ABILITY DIDN'T LAST.
VTUBERS STARTED TAKING THE WORLD BY STORM, AND NATURALLY I LEARNED ABOUT THEM TOO.
KiZUKE YAi
8888888
8888888888
So cute!
Amazing!!
Kyunkyuun!
MY WORLD WAS ROCKED TO ITS CORE.

EVERY-THING UNFURLED, SHOWING ME A REAL-ITY I'D BEEN BLIND TO.
NOW THE WORLD OUTSIDE IS A WHOLE NEW WORLD, ONE I CAN'T UNSEE.
DAD FAIR
FATHER
Dad Sensation
THIS IS MY LIFE NOW.

THREE MONTHS BEFORE THEIR WORLDS COLLIDED

My Dad's the Queen of All VTubers?!

FIGURED I'D BUY YOU SOME GEAR, HELP YOU GET ALL SET UP!
ALSO, I'VE BEEN HARD AT WORK COMING UP WITH AN AVATAR FOR YOU, TOO! ☆
AVATAR
HUH?!
NOT HAPPEN-ING!
I'M NOT INTERESTED, YOU OLD FART! I WANT YOU TO QUIT ALREADY!
DAMN IT... BUT HOW ELSE ARE WE GONNA PAY THE BILLS?
ALRIGHT, TAKE A LOOK!
I STAYED UP ALL LAST NIGHT DRAFTING THIS UP.
YOKUYA LUNA
Howdy, pyon!
HUU UUU UUU UUU UH?!
•Verbal tic (Pyon!)
•Tsundere attitude (Loves her family, but would never admit it)
•A Lunarian Hybrid
and a Lunaria
the moon
•Special A
The PyonPyon
BROAD 3 CAST

TH-THIS IS SUP-POSED TO BE ME?!
WHEEZE
C'MON, SON! GIVE ME AN "OKAAAY, PYON!" ❤
TRY IT!
SHUT UP!
Howdy, pyon!
HOLD ON, WHAT'S WITH THIS PART?! DID YOU WRITE SOME KIND OF TWISTED WISH FULFILLMENT INTO MY CHARACTER?!
LUNA
• VERBAL TIC (PYON!)
• TSUNDERE ATTITUDE (LOVES HER FAMILY, BUT WOULD NEVER ADMIT IT)
• A LUNARIAN HYBRID (DAUGHTER OF A HUMAN AND A LUNARIAN FROM THE MOON)
WE BOTH KNOW IT'S TRUE, SON.
I'M NOT A TSUNDERE!!
THE FACT THAT IT'S A GOOD ILLUSTRATION ACTUALLY PISSES ME OFF MORE.
THANKS, DAD! I HATE IT!

BY THE WAY... LUNA-PYON IS YAI-KYUN'S LITTLE SISTER!
KYUN!
WEL-COME TO THE WORLD, LITTLE SIS! ☆
YOU'RE IN YOUR FORTIES, OLD MAN. THERE'S NO WAY YOU HAVE A TEEN SISTER.
...THIS IS CURSED... I CAN PICTURE IT NOW...
HEWWO, KYUUUN! ☆ IT'S YAI TIME! ☆
IT'S A KYUN-TASTIC DAY, EVERYONE! I WANTED TO INTRODUCE YOU ALL TO MY LITTLE SISTER! ☆
EHEHEHEHEHE
I'M LUNA, PYOOOON! I HOPE WE GET ALONG, PYON! ❤

HEY HEY, LUNA. WOULD YOU LIKE TO COME OVER TO MY ROOM AND HANG OUT SOMETIMES?
I-I GUESS... JUST TO KILL TIME! IT'S NOT LIKE I WANT TO HANG OUT OR ANYTHING! ❤
GEEZ! YOU'RE SUCH A... TSUNDERE! ☆
HOW HORRIFYING...CAN I REALLY DO THIS? I CAN'T ...
WHY DOES IT FEEL LIKE THIS IS A MASSIVE DIVERGENT POINT IN MY LIFE?
WILL TAKASHI BE ABLE TO HOLD ON TO THE LAST REMAINING DREGS OF HIS DIGNITY?
TUNE IN NEXT TIME TO SEE THE (ONE-SIDED) CLASH BETWEEN FATHER AND SON!

Pyon!
AT THIS RATE I'M GONNA END UP AS A RABBIT-EARED TSUNDERE, I CAN'T LET IT HAPPEN!
I NEED TO TURN HIM DOWN!
MAN, THIS IS SO GREAT.
WHEN I WORKED AT THE OFFICE, I ALWAYS HAD TO PRETEND I WAS SOME-ONE I WASN'T.
I STARTED VTUBING SINCE I THOUGHT IT COULD BE FUN...
BUT NOW YOU KNOW ABOUT IT, AND I'M GLAD THAT I DON'T NEED TO HIDE MY TRUE SELF ANY LONG-ER...
IT REALLY WARMS MY HEART THAT YOU WANT TO DO THIS WITH ME.
THANKS, SON...FOR ACCEPTING ME AS I AM. I'M REALLY PROUD OF YOU.
ARE YOU KIDDING ME?!

OH COME ON...IF I SAY NO NOW, I'LL LOOK LIKE ONE OF THE BAD GUYS!
YEA
NAY
CURSE YOUR TYPE O BLOOD, DAD! CURSE IT TO HELL!
I'LL AT LEAST BUY MYSELF SOME TIME ...
M-MIGHT TAKE A WHILE TO MAKE A MODEL, RIGHT? MAYBE WE SHOULD TABLE THIS FOR NOW ...
NOPE! THE MODEL'S READY!
FWIP
BRUH.
HE'S FILLED IN THE MOAT, IT'S OVER!
TAKASHI'S CASTLE IS UNDER SIEGE!
NO! I'D RATHER DIE THAN LET HIM WIN! LISTEN, DAD! I—
OH, ALSO ...

WE CAN RAKE IN A LOT MORE MONEY FROM ADS IF WE GET ENOUGH VIEWERS.
WE'LL SPLIT THE PROFITS 50/50, SINCE WE'RE PARTNERS AND ALL!
TAKASHI'S CASTLE STATUS: PYON-QUERED
I GUESS YOU'RE RIGHT, DAD! I'M READY!
LET'S DO IT!
HIS LUST FOR MONEY WON OUT.
SWEET! I'M GLAD YOU AGREED, SINCE I ALREADY SET THE COLLAB DATE FOR THIS WEEKEND.
HUH?!
WHY AM I NOT SUR-PRISED ...
STARE
ACK!

I MEAN UH...O... OKAAAY, PYON! ❤
WOW!!
THAT'S SOME SERIOUS KYUN-KYUN ENERGY, SON!
UN KO
THE THEME OF OUR VIDEO WILL BE "SISTERLY INTIMACY," SO LET'S GET SOME PRACTICE IN!
HUFF...
PUFF...
AUUUUUUGH!!
COME TO PAPA YAI-KYUN!! I WANT A BIIIG HUG!
AAAAAAAA
NOOOOOOOOOOOOO!!
TAKASHI SOLD HIS SOUL TO THE DEVIL.
LITTLE DID HE KNOW OF THE HORROR THAT THIS WOULD ULTIMATELY UNLEASH.

THE DAY OF THE COLLAB STREAM HAS FINALLY ARRIVED!
HOW'S THE MOTION LAG?
NOT BAD.
IT'S KINDA INTER-ESTING, TO BE HONEST...
I STILL DON'T THINK I SHOULD BE DOING THIS... GUH...
I EVEN HAD TO BAIL ON SOME FRIENDS BY FAKING BEING SICK.
THAT BLOWS...
MAN, SERIOUSLY?
IT FEELS A LITTLE WEIRD, SNEAKING AROUND LIKE THIS WITH DAD.
BRRRRR
HUH?
?!

W-WAIT, ISN'T THAT TAKA-SHIMIZU-SAN?!
HUH?! THEY'RE WITH GIRLS?! WHAT?!
GLARE
Hey dude, you feeling better? We ran into Yasu's gf so we're just vibing for now. Takashimizu-san's
she said she
Takashi's (real-world) Crush
Takashimizu Maki
YOU'RE TELLING ME I MISSED THE CHANCE TO HANG OUT WITH HER...
ALL FOR THE SAKE OF DOING THIS WEIRD STUFF WITH MY DAD?!
WIGGLE WIGGLE
!
!

WE'RE AT YASU'S HOUSE NOW.
WE'RE GONNA WATCH KIZUKE YAI'S BROADCAST, DON'T FORGET TO TUNE IN.
OH NNNNNNNNNOOOOOOOOOOOOOOOOOO!!
IT'S TIME FOR YOUR BIG DEBUT, LUNA-PYON!
YANK
HUH?!
WAIT-
3
2
1
DIVE!

HIHI AND HEWWO, EVERYONE! IT'S TIME FOR EVERYONE'S SWEETIE, YAI! DID YOU MISS ME? KYUN-KYUUUN! ☆
TODAY'S A REALLY SPECIAL DAY, EVERY-KYUN! MY LITTLE SISTER'S HERE, KYUUUN! DO YOU WANNA MEET HER? ☆
TADAH! HERE SHE IS, KYUN! YOKUYA LUNA! ☆
H... HELLO EVERY-PYON...
WOW! YAI HAS A SISTER?!
THAT'S INTER-ESTING.
WISH I COULD SEE THE LOOK ON TAKASHI'S FACE.

I CAN'T DO THIS...
WHAT AM I DOING ...?
THE GIRL I LIKE IS ON THE OTHER SIDE OF THE SCREEN... HAPPILY WATCHING ME BEING FELT UP BY MY DAD...
CAN'T AFFORD TO GET DOXXED, THOUGH. I NEED TO STAY IN CHARACTER ...
GOTTA DO IT LIKE THE PROS DO. JUST GRIN AND BEAR IT, TAKASHI!
BEEP
YOU NERVOUS, SON? JUST SMILE, IT'LL START FEELING BETTER! ☆
CRINGE LEVELS ...
REACHING CRITICAL MASS...!
SMILE

WOW, LOOK AT THEM GO!
PROD
PROD
THEY'RE LIKE, JUST AS LOVEY-DOVEY AS WE ARE! HAHA!
PROD PROD PROD PROD PROD PROD PROD PROD PROD PROD PROD
HEY MAKI, YOU INTO KIZUKE YAI?
YES! I THINK SHE'S GREAT!
I HEARD A RUMOR SHE MIGHT BE SOME OLD DUDE, THOUGH!
NO WAY, I DON'T BELIEVE THAT FOR A MOMENT.
KIZUKE YAI EXUDES THE AURA OF A TRUE WOMAN. I JUST KNOW IT.

I THINK SHE'S REALLY AMAZ-ING.
I'M PRETTY JEALOUS OF THAT SISTER, I WISH I COULD BE CLOSE TO HER LIKE THAT.
LOVEY-DOVEY KYUN! ☆
IDOLS... NO, ANYONE WHO WORKS IN THE PUBLIC EYE MUST HAVE INCREDIBLE FORTITUDE...
BEING ABLE TO SMILE INSINCERELY SURE IS A SUPER-POWER...
TAKASHI DEVELOPED HIS ABILITY TO POWER THROUGH EMOTIONALLY TAXING SCENARIOS.

WE'LL KEEP UP THE GOOD WORK FROM HERE ON! PLEASE KEEP ROOTING FOR US, EVERY-KYUN! ☆
PYON-PYO-PYOOOON! (SCREAMS INTERNALLY)
FOOO!
TAKASHI'S SUFFERING WAS ENOUGH FUEL TO GENERATE OVER 300,000 VIEWS.
HIS TEARS WERE NOT VISIBLE ON HIS AVATAR.
RUB
RUB
AT THE VERY LEAST, HE WAS THANKFUL FOR THAT.
OH THIS IS TOTAL BULL!
NOW THERE'S SOME NEW BITCH CALLED LUNA ON THE SCENE?!
PYON!
BROADCAST#3: END

My Dad's the Queen of All VTubers?!

HIMURO MIZUKI (16)
I HAVE A SECRET THAT NOBODY CAN EVER KNOW.
IN TRUTH...
I'M A POPULAR VTUBER NAMED X-TA-SY!!
Sy-sama!!
POGGERS
This is where the fun begins
Let's party.
QUEEN!!
OOOOOH!!
I'm ready!
AND I HAVE ANOTHER SECRET ON TOP OF THAT ONE, TOO...!
(Special Broadcast: His Unhinged Passions)
I LIKE TO STREAM... BUCK NAKED!!

There's nothing like it!
THEY SING MY PRAISES IN THE DIGITAL WORLD, BUT NONE OF THEM KNOW...
Sy-sama!!
Y-You're stunning...
Marry me, Queen!
GORGEOUS!!!
I'M HERE TO HANG OUT...
WITH MY WANG OUT!!
SLAP SLAP SLAP
SLAP SLAP SLAP
HAAAAAAAAAAH!!

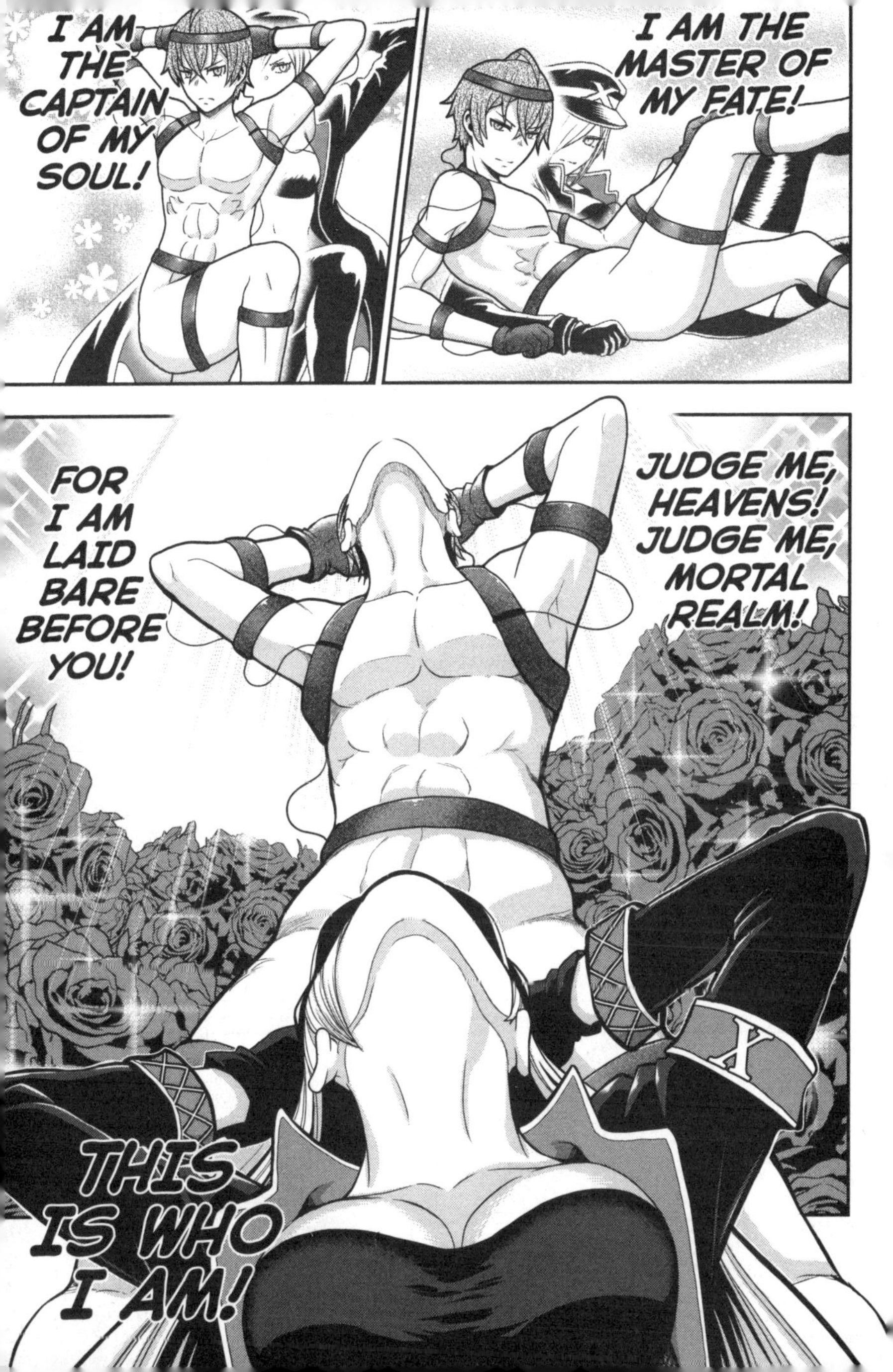
I AM THE MASTER OF MY FATE!
I AM THE CAPTAIN OF MY SOUL!
JUDGE ME, HEAVENS! JUDGE ME, MORTAL REALM!
FOR I AM LAID BARE BEFORE YOU!
THIS IS WHO I AM!

I love you, Sy-sama!
Hell yeah...
THIS IS MY ...
Nice pose!
BASED GODDESS!
Ecstasy!!
ECSTASSSSYYYYYY!!!!
HELL YEAH!
HNNNNNNGH!!
Queen confirmed.
NUT!!!
8888888888888
Look this way!!
ECSTASY!!
888888888
ASY!!
All together, bros!
888888888888
Ecstasy!!!
You're awesome, Sy-sama!!
Ecstassssy!!!
ACHOO!
YOU CATCH A COLD, TAKASHI?
YOU COULD DEFINITELY USE A FEW MORE LAYERS.

My Dad's the Queen of All VTubers?!

Gramps!
Virtual Grandpa!
Sup Oldie.
de, right? Gotta be a middle-aged dude.
GRAMPY!!
Don't cry, little gramps!
hing this old dude gives me life LMAO
Virtual Grand
Sup Oldie.
You're a dud
GRAMPY!!
Don't cry, litt
Gramps!!
He's gonna b
SEETHE
SEETHE
MOM, NO!!
SCREEEECH
WHO'S AN OLD DUDE, HUH?! QUIT CALLIN' ME GRAMPS, YOU LITTLE SHITS!!
BROAD 4 CAST
MOM, YOU'RE CHUGGING BEER AND SNACKING ON MIXED NUTS WITH YOUR MOUTH OPEN...
SCREW THIS!
FREAKS... I'M A LADY, DAMN IT! I OOZE FEMININE CHARM OUT MY ASS!!

I'VE NEVER ACTUALLY WATCHED ONE OF HER STREAMS,
GUESS I'LL TUNE IN.
BUT MAN, IS MOM REALLY COMING OFF AS A GUY?
UGH... THIS IS STRESS-IN' ME OUT...
HM?
OH, SHE'S LIVE AL-READY.
LIVE
OH CRAP, SHE DOESN'T KNOW SHE'S LIVE!
I NEED TO WARN HER!
GLUG GLUG
A LITTLE DRINKY OUGHTA SETTLE MY NERVES...

FWA AAAAH!!
MAN, THAT HITS THE SPOT! NOTHIN' LIKE A GOOD BEER.
HOLY SHIT, SHE IS AN OLD MAN!
CHECK YOUR PHONE ALREADY!
HM?
HUH?! SERI-OUSLY?! CRAP!
DING-A-LING!
GHH, GOTTA AMP MYSELF UP!
ズィヤ!
Hup!
SHE'S NOT HELPING HER IMAGE AT ALL!
KYURU-RIN! KYURU-RIN! HEWWO ALL!
IT'S YOUR LOVELY ARCH-ANGEL, TEKA-RIN-
UWU ...HRK!!
OH GOD... PLEASE NOT NOW ...
N-NOT WHEN I'M TRYING TO BE GIRLY ...

BRAAAP!!
GOD DAMN IT, THAT WAS THE BEER'S FAULT!! THIS IS BULL-SHIT!!
SHE REALLY IS JUST AN OLD GUY...
MY DAD'S SUPPOSED TO BE THE OLD GUY, NOT HER!
STRANGELY, TAKASHI'S MOM GAINED MORE SUB-SCRIBERS.
SHE NOW HAD A GRAND TOTAL OF 250 SUBSCRIBERS.

Grampy!!
Praise the Gramps!
Get up!! You gotta push it!!
Gramps!
Grampy!!
Gramps!
That's our gramps for ya!
Grampa!!
Grampy!!
Get up!! Yo
Gramps!
Grampa!!
Gramps!
Praise the
That's our
Grampy!!
TWITCH
TWITCH
TWITCH
GRAMPS... GRAMPS... GRAMPS...
I GET IT NOW... I REALLY AM AN OLD GUY...
MOM, NO!!
TWITCH
TWITCH
COME TO YOUR SENSES, GRAMPS!
WHUH?
I SAID COME TO YOUR SENSES, MOM!

MAYBE YOU COULD REBRAND WITH A MALE AVATAR…
NO WAY!
I WANT TO PROUDLY DISPLAY ALL MY WOMANLY BITS!!
DON'T EVER SAY THAT AGAIN, MOM.
YOU'LL HELP ME WORKSHOP MY CHARACTER AND MAKE HER MORE POPULAR, RIGHT?
UHH …
LET'S… HOW DO THE KIDS SAY IT… MAKE A REALLY 'HIP' AND 'WITH IT' CHARACTER!
YOUR MOM CAN BE PRETTY 'SWAG' TOO! PFFF!!
THAT DOESN'T HELP!!

DAMN IT...I'M JUST DOING THIS FOR MOM ...
MMM?
HEHEH. LOOKING TO BRANCH OUT INTO A SOLO CAREER ALREADY?
HM? WHAT MAKES A POPULAR CHARACTER?
TAKASHI'S ROOM
LIAR! TELL ME YOUR SECRETS !!
NO SECRET, SON. I'M JUST DOING WHAT I ENJOY DOING.
WHAT'S YOUR SECRET, DAD?
BUT IF YOU SWING TOO HARD AND MAKE YOUR CHARACTER TOO INTENSE, YOU'LL SCARE AWAY VIEWERS.
Reality
Dream
I THINK IT'S IMPORTANT TO GIVE YOUR CHARACTER A STRONG PERSONALITY.

IT CAN HELP IF YOU USE PEOPLE OR CHARACTERS YOU'RE FAMILIAR WITH AS INSPIRATION, TAKE CUES FROM THEM TO GUIDE YOUR VIRTUAL PERSONA'S BEHAVIOR.
THAT'S SOMETHING COMIC BOOK ARTISTS DO, TOO.
UN KO
OOOH!
SO WAIT, DAD. DID ANYONE IN PARTICULAR INSPIRE YOU TO CREATE YAI?
SCRIBBLE
SCRIBBLE
UN KO
WELL, ACTUALLY ...
YOUR MOM.
BLUSH!
SHE'S THE IDEAL WOMAN, AFTER ALL.
WHAAAT?! SO MOM'S BEEN COMPETING AGAINST HERSELF THIS WHOLE TIME?!
KIZUKE YAI
MOM (17)
JUST HOW DOES SHE LOOK IN DAD'S EYES?!

TRY TO DEVELOP A PERSONA YOU HAVE SOMETHING IN COMMON WITH, TOO.
FEMI-NINE FLAIR ♡
EVEN IF YOU MAKE AN OUTLANDISH CHARACTER, IT'LL BE EASIER TO PLAY THEM IF THEY SHARE AT LEAST ONE TRAIT WITH YOU.
FOR EXAMPLE, YOU AND LUNA-PYON BOTH HAVE TSUNDERE CHARACTER-ISTICS.
NO. NO WE DO NOT.
HMM ...
WHAT?
HMM... WHAT OTHER CHARACTER-ISTICS COULD WE USE...
OH YEAH, YOU MAKE A GREAT COMEDY STRAIGHT MAN!
Hey, hey, hey!!
SHUT THE HELL UP!

QUIT WASTING TIME AND GIMME MORE ADVICE!
WELL, IT'S DEFINITELY IMPORTANT TO SPEAK YOUR MIND WHEN SHAPING A CHARACTER.
VTuber Popularity Tips
① ADD A LITTLE CHARACTER.
(STRAIGHT
SQUEAK
SQUEAK
LUNA-PYON'S SUPER CUTE AND ALL, BUT I MADE HER MYSELF.
YOU SHOULD BE THE ONE TO DEVELOP HER PERSONALITY. TRY TO PICTURE AN IDEAL WOMAN.
AN IDEAL WOMAN, HUH...
THINKING OF SOMETHING HOT AND HEAVY, AREN'T YOU?
KA-LEWD!
THE HELL IS WRONG WITH YOU?!
WHAT MAKES YOU SAY THESE THINGS, DAD?!

I FOUND THE MAGAZINES UNDER YOUR BED, SON. I KNOW.
THAT'S NOT TRUE! THAT'S IMPOS-SIBLE!
ゴホ
COUGH!!
I DIDN'T LOOK TOO CLOSELY, SON.
BUT I MUST SAY, YOU HAVE GOOD TASTE.
GAA AAA AH!!
TAKASHI HAD A 'SPECIAL' KIZUKE YAI BOOK IN HIS COLLECTION.
JUST BE HONEST, SON.
Ufufufu...
I WENT THROUGH PUBERTY TOO, ONCE.
AUUUGH! SHUT UP!! SHUT UP, YOU IDIOT!!

OH RIGHT, YOU'RE GETTING USED TO THE GEAR BUT YOUR MOVEMENT'S STILL SUB-DUED.
GHH...
PEOPLE DON'T LIKE STIFFNESS. THEY WANT TO SEE A BROAD RANGE OF MOVEMENT.
SO I GUESS IF WE COMBINE THESE TO-GETHER...
VTuber Populari
①ADD A LITTLE C
(STRAIGHT MAN A
②GO LEWDER? TH
③MAKE MORE EX
THIS IS THE NEW AND IMPROVED LUNA-PYON!
HEY, HEY, HEY!!
WHAT THE HELL?! IS SHE A VARIETY SHOW ACT?!
WHAM

BAHA HAHA HA!!
THWACK
BASTARD! WERE YOU JERKING ME AROUND FROM THE START?!
IT'S ALL GOOD, SON. YOU'LL FIGURE IT OUT AS YOU GO.
TAKASHIIII? WANNA GET SOME SNACKS WITH ME? YOUR MOM'S GOT THE MUNCHIES!
CREAK
LET'S GRAB A SNACK AND COOL DOWN A BIT.
FINE, JERK. LET'S GO.
HM?
THINK SKIMPY
EXPRESSIVE M
MY GOD ...!

GUESS I CAN'T COUNT ON DAD FOR SOLID ADVICE HERE ...
MAYBE I CAN PICK UP SOME TIPS FROM WATCHING ANOTHER VTUBER ...
KYURURIN, KYURURIN! HEWWOOO ALL!
?!
HUH, MOM ?!
WHY'S SHE STREAMING?!
I'LL FOLLOW YOUR ADVICE, TAKASHI!!
VTuber Popularity Tips
① ADD A LITTLE CHARACTER.
(STRAIGHT MAN ACT WORKS)
② GO LEWDER? THINK SKIMPY CLOTHING.
③ MAKE MORE EXPRESSIVE MOTIO
I WON'T LET YOUR CAREFUL PLANNING GO TO WASTE! THANK YOU, SON!

BROADCAST #4: END

BROAD
5
CAST

WE ALL HAVE OUR SECRETS.
THIS RULE HOLDS TRUE IN THE SMALL SOCIETIES WITHIN SCHOOLS, TOO.
SOME HAVE SECRET CRUSHES ON THEIR CLASS-MATES.
AH! TAKASHI-MIZU-SAN!
THAT INCI-DENT'S STILL PRETTY RAW...
BUT IT'S NOT LIKE SHE KNOWS IT WAS ME.
TODAY'S THE DAY! I'M GONNA DO IT!
H-HEY, TAKASHIMIZU-SAN! THANK GOODNESS I RAN INTO-

AND SOME ...
AAAAHHHHHHH!
HAVE SECRET CRUSHES ON VIRTUAL GIRLS.
YOU'RE SO CUTE, YAI-KYUN ...

HUH?
AND A HARDCORE ONE AT THAT?!
TAKA-SHIMIZU-SAN'S A KIZUKE YAI FAN...?
RUB RUB RUB RUB RUB
SIGH... I WISH I COULD RUB UP TO THE REAL YAI-KYUN LIKE THIS...
MY 2D CRUSH IS MY DAD.
MY 3D CRUSH HAS A THING FOR MY DAD.
WHAT CURSED KARMA IS THIS?

I GUESS I CAN STILL TRY TALKING ...
H-HEY THERE, TAKA-SHIMIZU-SAN?
REACH
HUH?! TAKASHI-KUN?!
THERE'S BEEN A LOT OF SCREAMING IN MY LIFE LATELY ...
I'M SO EMBARRASSED YOU SAW ME LIKE THAT...
I-IT'S FINE, I'M SORRY I SCARED YOU.

UHM... ARE YOU A FAN OF KIZUKE YAI?
I AM, YES!
I THINK SHE'S A TRUE QUEEN, A GODDESS, IN FACT!
BUT SHE'S MY DAD ...
WHEN I FIRST SAW HER, I COULDN'T BELIEVE MY EYES!
SHE'S SO PRETTY, ISN'T SHE?!
BUT SHE'S MY DAD ...
I REALLY RESPECT HOW TRUE SHE IS TO HERSELF. SHE MOVES JUST LIKE A BEAUTIFUL GIRL EXPRESSING HER TRUE COLORS.
BUT. SHE'S. MY. DAD!

M-MAYBE I CAN DISPEL THE ILLUSION A LITTLE BIT...
HEY, UH, YOU EVER HEAR THE RUMOR THAT SHE MIGHT BE SOME OLD GUY?
I, UH, I MEAN ISN'T THAT A DUMB RUMOR?! IT'S SO FAKE!
WHOEVER STARTED IT IS PROBABLY JUST JEALOUS. THERE'S NO WAY SOMEONE AS GIRLY AS YAI COULD BE AN OLD GUY.
EXACTLY!
NICE SAVE!
SHE TOTALLY THOUGHT BADLY OF ME FOR A SECOND THERE!
SO UH, WHY KIZUKE YAI?

THERE'S A WHOLE WEALTH OF VTUBERS OUT THERE AND ALL.
YOU SHOULD CHECK THIS ONE OUT. SHE'S CALLED CRY TEKARI, AND–
I'M NOT INTERESTED.
OH, OKAY ...
I'M ONLY A FAN OF KIZUKE YAI! I DON'T FOLLOW ANYONE ELSE.
I ACTUALLY SENT A FEW MESSAGES TO HER THE OTHER DAY, AND...
SHE MADE A LITTLE PROMISE TO ME!
SHE DID?
HUH...?

THAT'S RIGHT! I ASKED IF I COULD TALK TO HER ABOUT SOME-THING ...
AND SHE SAID SHE'D MEET WITH ME THIS SUNDAY... IN THE FLESH!
SMACK
KYUN! ☆

W-WELL THAT'S A FINE "HOW-DO-YOU-DO!" WHAT WAS THAT FOR, SON?
SHUT UP, YOU WANNABE DIDDLER!
THOUGHT YOU COULD SLIDE INTO A HIGH SCHOOL GIRL'S DMS AND SECRETLY MEET WITH HER, DID YOU?!
EVEN MY DAD NEVER HIT ME WHEN I WAS GROWING UP!
WH-WHAT DO YOU EVEN MEAN?
?
LOOK, TODAY MY FRIEND SAID ...
THIS IS A TOTAL MISUNDER-STANDING! I SWEAR TO YOU THAT I'VE NEVER HAD EYES FOR ANYONE OTHER THAN YOUR MOTHER!
I'M KIZUKE YAI! I OFFER SUPPORT AND CARE FOR ALL YOUNG WOMEN! I'M A ROLE MODEL!

I'D SIMPLY DRESS UP AS A WOMAN AND MEET HER FOR THE CONSULTATION, THEN COME HOME!
HOWDY-HO!
ARE YOU STUPID?!
I DIS-APPROVE OF THAT PLAN ON MORAL AND AESTHETIC GROUNDS!
HM, IF YOU FEEL THAT WAY ...
BUT I CAN'T JUST LEAVE HER HANGING, CAN I? SHE NEEDS ADVICE.
...
WAIT. I'VE GOT IT.
HM?

THE DAY ARRIVED ...
TWO HOURS EARLY... JUST IN CASE ...
SIGH... I KNEW IT... MAYBE THIS SHOULDN'T HAPPEN ANYWAY... IT WAS RUDE OF ME TO TRY AND MEET UP WITH HER IN REAL LIFE, WASN'T IT?! I'M SO STUPID! ACK... MAYBE SHE THINKS I'M A STALK-ER... I'M NOT! I'M JUST A BIG FAN!
I DON'T WANT TO BOTHER HER, THOUGH... AGH... WHAT IF MY FACE GETS ALL FLUSHED? I'D BE SO EMBAR-RASSED... OH, THIS IS SO TOUGH... I JUST WANT TO GET TO KNOW HER BETTER!
CLACK
SORRY TO KEEP YOU WAITING, TAKA-SHIMIZU-SAN.
FLINCH!
HM?! AH?!
KI-KI-KI-KI-
KI-KIZUKE YAI IN THE FLESH ?!

DING
TH-THAT'S ME...
KI-KIZUKE YAI! SO KYUN-TASTIC TO MEET YOU. ☆
I'LL KILL YOU, OLD MAN!!
TAKASHI! YOU CAN PLAY THE ROLE OF KIZUKE YAI!
HOW DOES THAT WORK?!
IF YOU'RE A FELLOW STUDENT, IT WON'T BE AS WEIRD.
THAT WON'T WORK, DAD. I DON'T HAVE A GIRL'S VOICE!
HEHEH. BUT YOU WILL, MY BOY! ☆

BEHOLD! A VOICE CHANGING MASK!
IT WAS ONE OF THE FIRST PIECES OF GEAR I EVER BOUGHT!
PLUS IT HIDES YOUR FACE, TOO! TWO BIRDS, ONE STONE! ☆
I HATE THAT YOU HAVE THIS KIND OF STUFF ON HAND SO EASILY, DAD!
S-SORRY I LOOK LIKE THIS.
N-NO, DON'T BE SORRY!
I SHOULD BE THE ONE APOLOGIZING! IT WAS SELFISH OF ME TO MEET YOU LIKE THIS!

HONESTLY, JUST MEET-ING YOU IS A DREAM COME TRUE.
I-I'VE BEEN A HUGE FAN OF YOURS FROM THE VERY START, YAI-SAN.
S-SORRY FOR BEING SO FOR-WARD, BUT...
I WANT TO SEE YOU DANCE! YOUR FIRST DANCE, TO BE MORE SPECIFIC...
HUH?!
TWITCH
AH CRAP! I DIDN'T GET ON THE BANDWAGON UNTIL LATER! I DON'T KNOW YAI'S EARLIEST DANCES!
WHAT DO I D-

EEP!
POP
POP!

Y-YAI-SAN? ARE YOU OKAY?!
F-FINE! COMPLETELY FINE!
WHAT THE HELL ARE YOU DOING, DAD?!
BZZT
DO YOU READ ME, TAKASHI?
THERE ARE SPEAKERS INSIDE THE MASK. LISTEN TO MY VOICE.
SPEAK WHAT YOU HEAR, AND COPY MY MOTIONS!
THIS IS NUTS, BUT...
HER EYES ARE BRIMMING WITH ANTICIPATION...

I'M GONNA DO IT!
THERE'S NO GOING BACK!
WOO OOO OOW!!
IT'S REALLY YOU! YOU'RE REALLY HERE! OH MY GOODNESS!!
THIS IS INCREDIBLE! IT'S AMAZING!
THE ACTUAL SITUATION
CHATTER
CHATTER

WOWIE!
YOU'RE THE REAL DEAL! THAT WAS SUBLIME, YAI-KYUN!
HUFF... Y-YEAH, I'M GOOD.
OH, SORRY! I GOT SO EXCITED! ARE YOU OKAY?
WHEEZE
WHEEZE
THE DANCE PRACTICE FROM THAT COLLAB REALLY CAME IN HANDY ...
WE'LL KEEP UP THE GOOD WORK FROM HERE ON! PLEASE KEEP ROOTING FOR US, EVERY-KYUN! ☆
PYON-PYO-PYOOOON! (SCREAMS INTERNALLY)
HM? WHAT'S THAT NOISE?
SO, UHM! WHAT DID YOU WANT ADVICE ON?!
OH, RIGHT!
ACTU-ALLY ...

I WANT TO BE-COME A VTUBER...
YOU WHAAAAAT?!
I GUESS I'M NOT ALL THAT SUR-PRISED...
IS THAT SO?
WOULDN'T A GIRL AS PRETTY AS YOU BE BETTER SUITED TO REAL LIFE MODELING?
N-NO WAY!
MY HOME LIFE IS PRETTY STRICT...
I CAN'T REALLY EXPRESS MYSELF AT HOME, MUCH LESS PURSUE ANY HOB-BIES...

THAT'S WHY IT WAS SUCH A SHOCK WHEN I SAW YOU FOR THE FIRST TIME.
I love you!
Yai-kyuuuun!!
IT WAS JUST... SIMPLICITY INNOCENT CUTENESS AND SIMPLICITY.
IT MADE ME YEARN FOR THE SAME THING.
BUT I DON'T REALLY KNOW ANYTHING ABOUT VTUBING...
THAT'S WHY I WANTED TO TALK ABOUT IT WITH YOU, FACE TO FACE.
WE'RE THE SAME, YOU AND ME.
HUH?
HUH?
I UNDERSTAND.

I SPENT MANY LONG HOURS PRETENDING TO BE SOMEONE I'M NOT.
THAT'S WHY I STARTED ALL OF THIS TO BEGIN WITH.
BUT I KEPT IT HIDDEN FROM MY FAMILY.
BUT ONE DAY I GOT CAUGHT ...
OH.
AND THE ONE WHO FOUND ME OUT TIMIDLY CAME TO ME WITH THIS TO SAY:
This is incredible! I want to learn about streaming too! Please teach me how!
YOU CAN'T JUST FAKE MEMO-RIES LIKE THAT, DAD!

THEY ENDED UP SHOWING ME UNDER-STANDING AND COMPASSION.
WHEN DID I DO THAT?!
THEY ACCEPTED ALL THE PARTS OF ME I'D BEEN AFRAID TO SHOW THEM.
I DON'T THINK I DID!
IT CAN BE HARD TO BE A KID NOWADAYS, ESPECIALLY WHEN YOU HAVE A LOT RIDING ON YOUR SHOUL-DERS.
SO MANY PEOPLE THINK EXPRESSING THEMSELVES IS A BAD THING, OR THEY JUST DON'T EVEN KNOW WHERE TO START.
BUT HERE'S MY ADVICE TO YOU. DO WHAT MAKES YOU FEEL BEST. LIVE YOUR BEST LIFE.
I WILL!
I'M GLAD I CAME TO MEET YOU.
SQUEEZE

THANK YOU SO VERY MUCH! I'LL TAKE EVERY-THING YOU SAID TO HEART!
R-RIGHT...
MM... I GUESS IT ALL WORKED OUT?
IT ALMOST FELT LIKE A DATE THERE, SORTA...
I HOPE TAKASHIMIZU-SAN DOES HER BEST.
I'VE HAD PLENTY OF BAD EXPERI-ENCES, TOO.
BUT THAT ADVICE DAD GAVE WAS REALLY GOOD. MAYBE, JUST MAYBE... HE'S A GOOD VTUBER...

THAT'S RIGHT, WE'VE GOT HIM. MHM. SUS- PECTED PEEPING AND PUBLIC DISTURBANCE.
HE'S COMING ALONG VOLUN- TARILY.
NOOOOOOOOO!
POLICE
DAAAAAAAAD!!
BUT HE'S CERTAINLY NOT THE BEST DAD.
Statio
BROADCAST #5: END

My Dad's the Queen of All VTubers?!

HEY, DAD.
HM?
WHAT THE HECK? WHY'D YOU CALL ME UP IF YOU'RE NOT HERE ...
(Special Broacast: A Sneaky Story)
WHAT'S THIS?
TAKASHI.
I SUDDENLY HAD TO GO AND DO SOMETHING, BUT I LEFT ENOUGH GEAR BEHIND FOR A SOLO PERFORMANCE. TRY TO MAKE THE BEST OF IT!
WHAT AN IDIOT ...
AFTER HOW CRINGEY THE FIRST TIME WAS, WHY WOULD I DO IT AGAIN?
WHO'D WANNA BE A PRETTY GIRL, ANY-WAYS?!
NOT ME!
WHO'D FIND FUN IN BEING FAWNED OVER?
WHO GIVES A CRAP ABOUT THAT STUFF, HUH?!

NOT ME...
NOT ME AT ALL...
THIS IS JUST A TACTICAL DECISION...
IN WAR IT'S IMPORTANT TO KNOW THY ENEMY.
I'M NOT LIKE DAD. I'M NOT DOING HIS WEIRD THING.
I'M NOT EVEN STREAMING. THIS IS FINE.
LIVE
?!
HUH?! I'M STREAMING RIGHT NOW?!
FUSS
FUSS
HOW DO I TURN IT OFF?!
Oho!
Luna-pyon!
Pog!
Finally!!
WH-WHAAAAT?!

CRAP, THEY'RE HAPPY TO SEE ME...
WELL, WHAT-EVER. IT'S NOT LIKE I CARE OR ANY-THING.
What a pose!
H-HOW ABOUT THIS POSE?
You're so precious, Luna-
IS IT CUTE? AM I CUTE?
GH...WHAT IS THIS FEELING...
Luna-pyon!! <3
Looking good, newbie!
I'M A LITTLE FRUSTRATED, BUT...IT'S FUN...?
Turn this way, girl!
IS THIS THE POWER... OF BEING A CUTE GIRL?
OOOOOOH
HM?
So good!
美
What a sexy neck-nape!!
Nice
MY NAPE?
HOW CAN THEY SEE THE BACK OF MY NECK?

AH...
Step 1: Lay the bait
Step 2: Hide
Step 3: Remotely activate the stream and comment in chat
JUST ACCORDING TO PLAN. ☆

My Dad's the Queen of All VTubers?!

(Special Broadcast: Mom's Day Out)

RUSTLE
RUSTLE
SWISH
POKE
Vrrr rrrrr
KYURURIN! KYURURIN! HEWWO ALL!
YOUR LOVELY ARCHANGEL, TEKARIN, IS HERE TO ANSWER ALL YOUR QUESTIONS!
LIVE

How do you spend your mornings?
I'M A LIGHT SLEEPER, AND I WAKE UP NICE AND EARLY!
ONCE I'M UP, I MAKE IT MY MORNING RITUAL TO HAVE A LOVELY CUP OF TEA!
RING
RING
RING
RING
RINGRING RING
WHAM
ENOUGH ALREADY!

UGH... HEAD HURTS ...
DRANK WAY TOO MUCH LAST NIGHT CELEBRATING TAKASHI'S TEST RESULTS, HUH...
WELL, I WAS CELEBRATING THE FACT THAT MY DIET'S BEEN WORKING A BIT, TOO...
UGHH...
RATTLE
THE BEST CURE FOR A HANGOVER ...
ENERGY
SWISH
IS A MORNING BEER!
Whew!

CLATTER
7:30 am
WE GOT CURRY FOR BREAKFAST, BOYS.
JUST FIGURED WE COULD GET RID OF LAST NIGHT'S LEFTOVERS.
YUMMY!
BUT HEY, CURRY AND HOTPOT ARE GREAT BECAUSE YOU CAN REUSE THEM FOR MULTIPLE MEALS, RIGHT?
THAT'S THE KIND OF LOGIC USED BY OLDER SINGLE MEN ...
ALRIGHT I'M HEADING OUT.
I'LL TAKE CARE OF MY ERRANDS, TOO. GOOD LUCK AT WORK, DEAR.
I'LL BE OFF THEN, SWEETIE.
SNEAK
BYE BYE!
SEE YOU LATER!

Do you have a job?
OF COURSE NOT! I'M A PRECIOUS PRINCESS!
I WOULD NEVER TOIL, WORK, OR SWEAT.
11:30 am
HAH!
WHAM
BAM
SLAM

FWOOOOOOO
S-SUCH POWER ...
I GUESS THE RUMORS ARE TRUE AFTER ALL ...
SIGH
DAMN, I'M RUSTY.

ALRIGHT, LET'S TAKE A BREAK.
YES SENSEI!
HEY, NASAKENAKA! WORKING HARD?
TWITCH
AH, YES SENSEI! I'M TRY-ING!
BUT I DON'T KNOW IF IT'S WORTH IT... I FEEL LIKE I'M GOING NOWHERE ...
SHUFFLE
FOOL!
EVERYONE'S INEXPERI-ENCED AT THE START, KID!
THAT'S WHY YOU KEEP GOING! LITTLE BY LITTLE YOU'LL GET BETTER, 'TIL YOU HAVE REAL LONG-TERM GAINS!
Y-YES SENSEI! I'LL DO MY BEST!

I WAS JUST LAUGHING AT THIS DUMB GUY. HE'S CALLED CRY TEKARI.
DO YOU KNOW ABOUT VTUBERS?
SNICKER
OH YEAH, WHAT WERE YOU LOOKING AT?
O-OH UHM...
CRACK
THINK FAST, YOU WORTHLESS MAGGOT!!
S-SENSEI?!

King Karate
THANK YOU, SIR!
LATER, GUYS!
PING
Do you have any hobbies?
HOBBIES? OH! I LOVE COOKING!
COOKING IS A WOMAN'S PASSION, AFTER ALL!

CHA-CHING
THAT'LL BE 3,280 YEN PLEASE.
CREAK
I'M BACK!
WELCOME HOME, HUN. DINNER'S READY.
HE'S BEEN GETTING HOME EARLIER THAN ME LATELY.
I WONDER IF HIS WORKFLOW CHANGED UP.
NOT THAT I'M COMPLAINING. IT'S NICE TO SEE HIM WHEN I GET HOME.

I'M BACK...
I'M PRETTY WORN OUT TODAY... SORRY ...
I'M ON COOKING DUTY TODAY, SILLY.
YOU CAN PUT YOUR FEET UP.
IF YOU ASK ME, DAD MAKES THE BEST STUFF, SO I'M FINE WITH THAT.
GLARE
NO WAY, MY COOKING CAN'T COMPARE TO THE HEARTY CURRY YOUR MOM WHIPS UP.
BON APPÉTIT, YOU TWO!
MY HUSBAND IS TOTALLY WIFE MATERIAL!
SPARKLESPARKLE

HELL YEAH!
YAHOO
I LOVE SEEING YOU SMILE, DEAR!
MM... THAT WAS SO GOOD...
MAN, THAT WAS A FEAST! GUESS WE CAN TAKE IT EASY FOR THE EVENING.
YEP.
SURE, I'LL GO RELAX A BIT.
I APPRECIATE THAT MY FAMILY VALUES INDIVIDUAL SPACE.
WE EACH GET SOME TIME TO DO OUR OWN THING FOR A COUPLE HOURS AFTER DINNER.

ALRIGHT, TODAY'S THE DAY!
RUSTLE
RUSTLE
JUST GOTTA GET ALL THE GEAR READY.
OPEN THIS BOX TO DIE INSTANTLY!
I WONDER IF TAKASHI WILL HELP ME OUT TODAY...
IT'S KINDA CRAZY HOW MUCH HE KNOWS ABOUT THIS STUFF.
Takashi
Can you help me VTube today?
た
Sorry. I'm a little occupied.
OH WELL, NO WORRIES.
TAKASHI SURE HAS BEEN A LOT BUSIER LATELY...
HE IS AROUND THAT AGE, THOUGH... **MAYBE HE'S HIDING A GIRL-FRIEND FROM ME!** I WONDER IF HE'S GOTTEN PAST THE CUDDLING STAGE YET...

MEANWHILE IN TAKASHI'S ROOM.
CUDDLE CUDDLE
LET'S DO ANOTHER COLLAB VIDEO, SON! C'MOOON!
NOO OOO OOO OO!!
ANOTHER THING I'M THANKFUL FOR IS OUR THICK WALLS.
I DON'T KNOW WHY MY HUSBAND SUDDENLY HAD THEM SOUND-PROOFED ABOUT HALF A YEAR AGO, BUT IT SURE CAME IN HANDY.
FWIP
NOW I CAN FOLLOW MY DREAMS.
WHEN I PUT ON THE VIRTUAL GEAR, I'M REBORN...

I BECOME A SUPER-PRINCESS! A TOTAL CUTIE PIE!
KYURURIN! KYURURIN! HEWWO ALL!
YOUR LOVELY ARCHANGEL, TEKARIN, IS HERE TO ANSWER ALL YOUR QUESTIONS!
AND MY WHAT A DAY! QUITE THE ELEGANT ONE, IF I DO SAY SO MYSELF!
I TOOK A GREAT MANY PHOTOS, TOO! CERTAINLY ENOUGH FOR SCRAP-BOOKING!

How many times do we have to teach you this lesson, old man?!
Gramps!
OK Boomer. I totally beli
LOL
WH-?!
NOOO! YOU CAN'T JUST CALL ME AN OLD MAN!!
BASTARDS! WHAT'S THE PROBLEM THIS TIME?! QUIT IT!
CLATTER
HIC!

MAN, THIS IS A WHOLE LOAD OF BULL…
WHY DO I GAIN SUBSCRIBERS EVERY TIME I YELL AT THEM?
I TOLD 'EM TO STOP CAL-LING ME GRAMPS, GEEZ…
SWISH
I THOUGHT YOU'D BE COLD, SWEETIE.
D-DARL-ING!
I'M NOT ALL THAT COLD…
DID YOU HAVE A GOOD DAY?
I DID. I'M ALL DONE WITH (VTUBING) WORK FOR THE DAY.

I THOUGHT I'D COME AND SPEND SOME TIME WITH YOU.
FEELING UP FOR A LITTLE DATE, MIKOKO-CHAN?
KAORU-SAN...
ADULTS HAVE MANY SIDES TO THEM.
THEY HAVE THEIR WORK FACE.
THEIR FAMILY FACE.
EVEN THEIR VIRTUAL FACE. THEY ALL MAKE UP PART OF THE TRUE PERSON.

AND, JUST FOR A WHILE...
CLINK
THESE TWO COULD ENJOY A SIDE OF EACH OTHER THAT ONLY THEY KNEW.
THE NEXT TIME...
THE HELL DO YOU MEAN BY "YOU REMIND ME OF KADONO TAKUZO"?! HE WAS BORN IN THE 1940s, YOU LITTLE SHIT!!
MOM NOOOO!!
GROW UP A LITTLE!!
END

APPOPO
サッポポ生ビール
黒ラベル

My Dad's the Queen of All VTubers?!

IT'S FINE, MAN! WE WENT TO THE SAME HIGH SCHOOL, RIGHT? LEND ME SOME CASH.
A COLLEGE FRESHMAN LIKE YOU OUGHTA HAVE LOTS OF SPARE POCKET CHANGE, RIGHT?
AH, NO, I, UH ...
(Special Broadcast: Back When...)
I, UH... I CAN'T REALLY ...
HUH? SPEAK UP, MAN! LOUDER!
Takashi's Dad (21)
C'MON, PUSSY. SPEAK UP.
STEP
STEP
STEP
EARTH TO SISSY. SPIT IT OUT AL-READY.
STEP
STEP
STEP
STEP
...
HUH?

HNGH!!
MI ...
AH ...
MIKOKO-CHAN!
FWOOSH
WH-WHAT WAS THAT ABOUT?!
OH GOSH, M-MASA-KUN! HE'S OUT COLD!
Takashi's Mom (16)
SIGH...

あああああAAAAAAAAH!!
OH CRAP! I OVER-DID IT!!
FLINCH
IF MY DAD FINDS OUT ABOUT THIS HE'LL KICK MY ASS!!
AND WHAT ABOUT YOU, BRO?! YOU'RE NOT A SMALL GUY, YOU SHOULD BE ABLE TO FIGHT BACK!
WHAT WOULD'VE HAPPENED IF YOUR INCREDIBLY TALENTED CHILDHOOD FRIEND HADN'T BEEN IN THE AREA BY CHANCE, HUH?!
S-SORRY...
MAN, I JUST DECIDED I WANTED TO BE AN IDOL, TOO... I CAN'T ACT LIKE THIS!
GOSH DARN IT!
HUH?
YOU'RE TRYING TO BECOME AN IDOL, MIKOKO-CHAN?
OH CRAP...

THAT'S AMAZING! I THINK YOU SHOULD GO FOR IT!
YOU'RE SPLENDID AND CHARMING IN ALL KINDS OF WAYS, MIKOKO-CHAN! I'LL ROOT FOR YOU!
GULP...
S-SPLENDID AND CHARM-ING, YOU SAY...?
I THINK YOU ONLY SEE MY GOOD SIDES, BRO.
IT'D BE NICE IF ALL IDOL FANS WERE LIKE YOU.
BUT YOU'RE PRETTY NAIVE, BRO. I'M A LITTLE WORRIED YOU'LL GET SUCKERED INTO AN EXPLOITATIVE COMPANY OR SOMETHING.
YOU GONNA BE OKAY?
D-DON'T SAY THINGS LIKE THAT...

BUT STILL ...
WHY DO YOU WANT TO BE AN IDOL, MIKOKO-CHAN?
MM ...
W-WILL YOU PROMISE NOT TO LAUGH?
TURN
SURE, I PROMISE.
I'VE ALWAYS WANTED TO BE LIKE A PRINCESS ...
BUT YOU KNOW MY FAMILY...IT'S A REAL GRUFF, MANLY HOUSEHOLD. I KNOW I'M NOT THE GIRLIEST... I HAVE A LOT OF CRASS PARTS TO ME.
I CAN FLY OFF THE HANDLE PRETTY EASILY, TOO.
I FIGURED THAT WAS JUST WHO I AM, THOUGH ...
BUT THEN, ONE DAY ...

I SAW A DOCUMENTARY ABOUT IDOLS ON TV!
CHEEEER!
THEY WERE REAL-LIFE PRIN-CESSES!
WHEN I SAW THAT, I THOUGHT...
WELL, I THOUGHT I COULD MAYBE BE THE PRINCESS I WANT TO BE, TOO.
BUT WHAT REALLY STOOD OUT WAS THAT THEY WEREN'T BORN AS PRINCESSES!
THEY WORKED SO HARD BEHIND THE SCENES TO MAKE THEIR DREAMS REAL!

SO I KINDA WANNA INSPIRE OTHERS IN THE SAME WAY, YOU KNOW?!
I WANT TO FILL A STADIUM WITH 100,000 SMILING PEOPLE!
THAT'S A LOVELY DREAM.
IF IT'S ALRIGHT, I'D LIKE TO BE YOUR VERY FIRST FAN, THEN.
TH...
THANKS ...
THINK FAST! HUP HUP HUP!
NUDGE
NUDGE
H-HEY! OWIE!
STILL, I THINK YOUR DREAM IS AMAZING ...

I WANT A FUTURE LIKE YOURS, MIKOKO-CHAN.
A BRIGHT AND SHINING ONE.
I THINK I WANT TO MAKE PEOPLE SMILE, TOO ...
CHEEEER!
POG!!
I'M YOUR BIGGEST FAN!
YAI-KYUN!
YAI-KYUN!
YOU'RE MY IDOL, YAI-KYUN!
LOLOLOL
IN ANY WAY I CAN!
YAI-KYUN!
END

My Dad's the Queen of All VTubers?!

THERE ARE LITTLE THINGS NOW...
OH MY, REALLY?
(Special Broadcast: Subtle Assimilation)
LITTLE WAYS HIS TONE OF VOICE GOES UP.
OH YEAH! I SAW THAT ONE~!
OH WOWIE, THAT'S DEFINITELY SOMETHING!
KYUN-KYUN! I KNOW, RIGHT?
UN KO
DON'T TELL ME HE'S MERG-ING WITH YAI?!

DAD, YOUR ONLINE PERSON-ALITY KEEPS SLIPPING OUT.
DIDN'T YOU SAY YOU WANTED TO KEEP IT HIDDEN FROM MOM?
SORRY, IT'S JUST A LITTLE HARD TO SWITCH OFF FROM WORK MODE WHEN I COME HOME.
DID YOU JUST SAY "COME HOME"?
YOU DON'T LEAVE THE HOUSE, DAD! THIS IS YOUR HOME! ARE YOU THAT BLIND?!
OF COURSE NOT, SON. IN FACT, IT WAS MY EYES BEING OPEN TO OUR HOUSEHOLD BUDGET THAT MADE ME GO DOWN THIS PATH TO BEGIN WITH.
POW!
REALITY
DAMN IT DAD, DON'T SWITCH THE SUBJECT!

SPEAKING OF BUDGETING, I'VE FOUND CUTE OUTFITS CATCHING MY EYE RECENTLY.
UFUFU...
KAWAII
KAWAII
I NEED TO CONSIDER WHICH ONES I'D LOOK BEST IN.
WELL, CLEARLY HE'S TOO FAR GONE!
I'M A FASHION ICON AND A ROLE MODEL FOR A LOT OF YOUNG GIRLS.
EVEN IN REALITY, I NEED TO KEEP AN EYE OUT FOR WHAT MIGHT WORK.
GAAAAAH...
HE'S WAY TOO COMMITTED TO HIS JOB!
LOOK, JUST REFLECT ON WHAT I SAID! YOU DON'T SEE IT, BUT YOU'RE ACTING MORE LIKE YAI!
HARRUMPH!
HEH...
LOOKS LIKE YOU HAVEN'T NOTICED, SON...
WHAT A HOPELESS BOY.

I'M NOT THE ONLY ONE...
WHO'S BEEN SUBTLY CHANGING.
TH-THIS IS JUST BECAUSE I DON'T WANT TO GET FOUND OUT, BY THE WAY!
HMPH!
I-IT'S NOT LIKE I'M WORRIED FOR YOU, OR ANY-THING!
UN KO
SURE THING, KYUN! ☆
DON'T TEST ME, DAMN IT!
WHOEVER FIGHTS MONSTERS SHOULD SEE TO IT THAT IN THE PROCESS HE DOES NOT BECOME A MONSTER. AND IF YOU GAZE LONG ENOUGH INTO AN ABYSS, THE ABYSS WILL GAZE BACK INTO YOU.
-FRIEDRICH NIETZSCHE

Author's Afterword

So, you picked up a book called **"My Dad's the Queen of All Vtubers?!"**, huh? Thank you very much, bud. **I appreciate it.**

This is my **first commercial work**, and it was all possible thanks to the great team of editorial staff and workers at the publishing office. I'm pretty pleased with it!

I gotta say though, **a lot of stuff** ended up happening along the way.

One such incident was my fault. I like to take **reference pictures of myself** for poses that are especially hard to draw. One time I accidentally **left some of these photos in the data** of the manuscript I sent over to my editor, and he stumbled upon it and didn't know what to think!

One of the photos had me in a really wild pose, too!

The entire editorial staff saw it!
They all laughed their asses off at me! I wanted to dig a really deep hole and hide in it forever!

But don't worry, I'll use that cringe as fuel for the furnace of creation! Only by discarding all of my shame can I work at my best!

Look forward to volume 2, folks! It's coming!

Translator's Afterword

Hello there! I'm Andrew Hodgson, the translator for **"My Dad's the Queen of All VTubers?!"**

Since you've read this far, I'm gonna assume the best and hope you've enjoyed reading it as much as I enjoyed translating it. **This title was like a breath of fresh air for me**, certainly the only project in recent memory that had me laughing throughout the entire translation process.

Right now it's ~11AM. I'm typing this from my living room after looking over the final pre-release draft of the manga, and I must say, I'm really happy with how it all came together. This manga immediately captured my attention, and also kicked off my dive into **VTuber culture** in general, so now I have even more excuses to procrastinate... orz

Anyways, enough prattling! What I really like about this book is that it feels like Wataru Akashingo managed to blend **total madcap comedy** with a **very specific type of discomfort** I'm sure we can all somewhat relate to. The dialogue was filled with a surprising roster of **references to obscure stuff** as well. For example, part of X-TA-SY's internal monologue was taken from a classic poem by the famous Edo-period samurai, Sakamoto Ryoma. The **"Don't fall for the siren song!"** line in Chapter 2 more literally meant something along the lines of "You look like the boy who wanted that trumpet!" After plenty of googling I traced this reference back to **some credit company commercial from 1986** about a young boy who gazed lovingly through a shop window at a trumpet.

On top of these, I had some run-ins with **stream chat comments like "03" in the JP** where connecting the dots to reach the analog of "Old Man" or "Gramps" ended up taking a bit sometimes. I kept thinking **"What does 03 mean...?"** until it eventually clicked and I yelled out **"OH! OSSAN!"** (old guy) one afternoon while washing the dishes. This combination of interesting, downright esoteric references along with modern internet slang ended up being quite the challenge, but luckily doing all that research was a whole lot of fun!

I don't wanna drone on for too long, so I'll call it here! Thanks for reading, and I look forward to seeing what people think! **It was nice to give a bit of my own perspective on all of this, and hopefully I'll see you all in volume 2 as well.**

My Dad's the Queen of All VTubers?!

Author: Wataru Akashingo

VOL. 1

OYAJI GA BISHOJO NI NATTETA HANASHI VOL. 1

First published by Futabasha Publishers Ltd., in 2019
English version published by Kaiten Books LLC.

For press inquiries or review copies, please send all correspondence to info@kaitenbooks.com

ISBNs: 978-1-952241-09-3 (paperback)
978-1-952241-08-6 (ebook)

Printed in Canada

First Printing: 2020

Translation
Andrew Hodgson

Editing
Christian Knoll

Cleaning and Redrawing
Maksym Osiejko

Typesetting
Christian Knoll
Kazushi Mizutani

Quality Assurance
Hendra Boerma

Production Manager
Garrison Denim

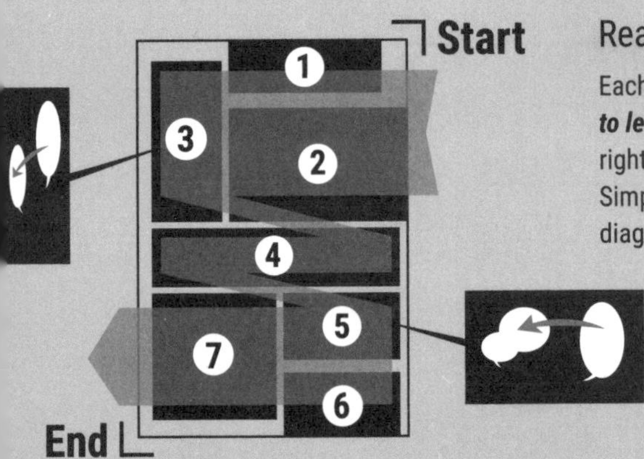

Reading Instructions:

Each page reads from ***right to left***; starting from the top right, ending at bottom left. Simple as that. Follow diagram on left.

Come visit us online at: www.kaitenbooks.com

My Dad's the Queen of All VTubers?!